the **GREAT** escape

the Magic Shop

the GREAT escape

Kate Egan
with Magician Mike Lane

illustrated by **Eric Wight**

FEIWEL AND FRIENDS

NEW YORK

A FEIWEL AND FRIENDS BOOK
An Imprint of Macmillan

Feiwel and Friends books may be purchased for business or promotional
use. For information on bulk purchases, please contact the Macmillan
Corporate and Premium Sales Department at (800) 221-7945 x5442
or by e-mail at specialmarkets@macmillan.com.

Library of Congress Cataloging-in-Publication Data Available

ISBN: 978-1-250-02916-4 [hardcover] / 978-1-250-04718-2 [paperback]
978-1-250-06421-9 [ebook]

Book design by Véronique Lefèvre Sweet

Feiwel and Friends logo designed by Filomena Tuosto

First Edition: 2014

1 3 5 7 9 10 8 6 4 2

mackids.com

For Louisa, Simon, and Frankie.
—K. E.

To my Mom, Dad, and sister, you were my very
first audience. Thank you for humoring me by watching
my magic shows, over and over and over. . . .
—M. L.

✷ Chapter 1 ✷
FOOD FIGHT

Lunchtime was over, and Mrs. Canfield wasn't happy.

Mike Weiss's class had just streamed up from the cafeteria, dropped their lunchboxes in a bin, and headed back to the classroom. Some kids were still talking and laughing, but Mike felt a chill in the air. Usually, Mrs. Canfield greeted everyone when they came back. She asked what was on the menu, or gave the

occasional high five. Today, she was standing at the door with her arms crossed.

Mrs. Canfield hadn't been on lunch duty, but she knew what had happened. Mike didn't need magic to figure that out.

Kids pulled their chairs back and settled into their desks. One by one, they noticed Mrs. Canfield, glaring. Suddenly, the classroom got really quiet.

On a normal day, Mrs. Canfield would be passing out papers to get ready for math.

On a normal day, she would clap her hands to settle everyone down.

Today, she watched and waited until they settled down on their own.

Mrs. Canfield's voice was low when she finally spoke. "Guys, we need to talk about appropriate behavior in the cafeteria. And I have to say, I'm a little disappointed. Do we really need to go over the basics? You're in

fourth grade now. I thought you knew better."

Nobody moved. Nobody spoke. Not even Mike.

"Can anyone tell me what happened?" Mrs. Canfield asked in a weird voice.

Emily raised her hand. "There was a food fight," she reported.

Other kids interrupted right away.

"It was not a food fight!" said Oscar.

"Yeah!" Lacey chimed in. "Someone threw food, and then there was a fight, but that's not the same. . . ."

Now, everyone was talking at once.

Mike drummed his fingers on his

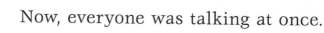

knees. He didn't like to get in trouble, but he also didn't like when it was about to happen to someone else. He always felt sorry for the kid on the spot. He knew what that was like.

Mrs. Canfield held up her hand. "Hang on," she said. Her voice was still quiet, but it felt like she was yelling. "This isn't going to work. Please take out a piece of paper and a pencil. I would like for each of you to write me a letter about what you just saw in the cafeteria."

Silently, everyone got out their supplies.

What had Mike seen at lunch? The inside of his PB&J, which he opened up and ate one side at a time. The face of his new friend, Adam, sitting across the table. Then there was a scoop of tuna fish, hurled at the wall. And a shriek from the kid standing next to it.

Some people rushed over and blocked his view of whatever happened next.

Mike was not involved.

He bit the eraser off his pencil and rolled it around on his desk. A food fight? he thought. Seriously? Who would even do that? He picked up the eraser and chewed it like a piece of gum. Jackson Jacobs, maybe. Or those twins from Nora's class, Tyler and Chase—they were bad news. He wasn't sure he should name names, though.

Mike looked up from his paper, his eyes darted around the room. Could anyone else be responsible?

His eyes met several other pairs of eyes. They, too, were trying to figure out who'd started trouble.

Trouble was, they were looking at *him*. Everyone thought it was Mike.

He looked down and raced through his letter. What else could he do?

Dear Mrs. Canfield,

I sat with Adam at lunch today. I showed him a card trick and ate a PB & J. I also noticed that there was a banana peel on the floor. Lucky that no one slipped on it. But it wouldn't be a good idea to throw it, either. That would be bananas.

your friend,

Mike Weiss

He slammed his pencil down. Now, more people were watching him. He scowled at them and said "It wasn't me, okay?" with his eyes.

Then Mr. Malone was there, knocking on the window of the classroom door.

Math tutoring was not exactly the highlight of Mike's day, but right now, he couldn't get there fast enough. His face was bright red as he walked past Mrs. Canfield's desk.

Mike was doing a little better in school these days. Learning magic helped him learn other things, too. If Mike practiced the same trick over and over, he'd get to the point where he could do it automatically. Who knew it was the same with spelling words?

He was even doing a little better about following school rules. Apparently, no one had noticed, though. The other kids just thought he was the same old Mike, always going to the principal. They thought he was bad news, too.

Today, Mr. Malone settled into his chair and rubbed his hands together like he was cold. "I thought we'd try something a little different this time," he said.

Mike slumped in his chair. "Are we starting fractions?" he asked. The rest of his class was almost done with that chapter.

Mr. Malone swept his hand dramatically over the papers in front of him. "Let's try some . . . mathematical magic," he suggested.

Mike smiled at him, maybe for the first time ever. Balding, skinny old Mr. Malone, in his yellow shirt that looked like plastic . . . when did he get so nice?

It was like he knew Mike's afternoon was off to a bad start. He was trying to cheer him up. He was trying to make a connection.

"Pick a number," the math tutor said. "A three-digit number, with all the digits different, and no zeroes."

"Um . . . okay," said Mike. "216?"

"Great," said Mr. Malone. "Next, reverse the number and subtract the smaller one from the bigger one."

"612 minus 216 . . ." Mike said. "Can I use a calculator?" Mr. Malone handed him a pad instead.

Mike wrote the number down, tried to remember regrouping, and got an answer. "612 minus 216 equals 396?" he said uncertainly.

"That's right!" said Mr. Malone. "Now reverse that number, too."

"693?" Mike asked. Where was the magic? he wondered.

Mr. Malone nodded. "Add it to the number you had before you reversed it." He pushed the pad back to Mike.

"693 plus 396 is . . ." Mike said, writing it all out.

Mr. Malone cut him off. "Don't tell me!" He closed his eyes, paused, and took a deep breath. "Is it 1089?"

"Yeah," Mike said, surprised. Wasn't he supposed to be the one doing the math?

Mr. Malone's eyes popped open. "Let's try it again," he said.

So Mike picked another random number. "542," he said.

"Reverse and subtract," prompted Mr. Malone.

Mike scribbled it on the pad. "542 minus 245 is . . . 297."

"Now reverse and add it to the number you had before you reversed."

Mr. Malone closed his eyes again, and Mike said, "No, let me do it this time."

He wrote it all out. 297 plus 792 was . . . 1089. Again.

"Hey, it's the same answer as last time!" Mike said.

Mr. Malone coughed. Or was he laughing? Oh, man . . . he was cracking himself up!

"It's always 1089," he told Mike. "Every. Single. Time."

Mike didn't think it was funny, exactly. But he did think it was pretty cool. He tried it with a bunch of other numbers, and it really worked.

"See?" the tutor said. "I knew you could do this math if I made it interesting."

"Magic definitely makes it interesting," Mike agreed. He even remembered to say thanks.

Mike didn't always keep up with the rest of his class. And yeah, he got in trouble sometimes.

He never did it on purpose, though. He just made a lot of mistakes. He was still a good kid, and he could even be a good student. If Mr. Malone could get it, why couldn't other people get it, too?

Mike would never start a fight. Or throw tuna fish at a wall. No matter what anyone else thought.

If only he knew a magic trick for changing his reputation.

Chapter 2
HOUDINI'S HAT?

Mike locked his bike in his usual place outside The White Rabbit. He put the key in his pocket and checked his watch. Eleven minutes. A personal best. He got to the magic shop a little faster every time he came.

What was he going to do when it was winter? Mike was pretty worried about that. He couldn't ride his bike through the snow, but there wasn't another way for him to get around on his own. It was hard enough to convince his parents that he could handle biking downtown.

For now, he had the best routine ever. On days that his parents were home after school—*and* his neighbor, Nora, was busy *and* he had no homework—he was allowed to bike to the magic shop alone. He had to call when he got there and call again when he was leaving. He had to get home before dark, too. Other than that, he could pretty much stay as long as he wanted.

Okay, it was never as long as he wanted. But if going to school was like crunching celery sticks, coming to The White Rabbit was like sucking down an extra-large chocolate milkshake: super-sweet.

The shop was warm and bright on this late-fall afternoon. Mr. Zerlin was standing near the counter, his hair sticking out in six directions, talking to a man in a Red Sox cap. He waved at Mike and said, "He's a friend." Was

Mr. Zerlin talking about the Red Sox guy? Or was he talking about Mike? The magician was always hard to understand. Still, Mike beamed.

Mr. Zerlin was holding a small box. He showed it to Mike and the guy in the cap, then opened it up to reveal a deck of cards inside. (Mike knew that he bought crates of them for the shop.) Mike could tell he was about to perform.

Mr. Zerlin handed the cards to the guy, nodded, and said, "You can shuffle them, Cam."

That was Mike's first clue that the guy in the cap might be more than a baseball fan who'd wandered in off the street. Was he a friend of Mr. Zerlin's?

His next clue was watching Cam shuffle. The cards moved so quickly, they were a blur, and he must have shuffled a dozen times before he handed the deck back to Mr. Zerlin. Whoa, thought Mike. Was there such a thing as a professional card player? If there was, this guy had to be one.

Mr. Zerlin took the cards and put them back in the box. He closed up the box. Then he lifted the box of cards and pressed it to his forehead, as if his brain could sense what was inside. He looked like he was meditating. Or concentrating. Finally, he looked at Mike and Cam and said, "In my mind's eye, I can see the first card in this deck."

Mike and Cam glanced at each other. "Yeah?" said Cam. His voice reminded Mike of the way his dad sounded when he'd stayed up too late. Dry and raspy.

"Seven of spades," said Mr. Zerlin.

"Cool trick," said Cam. Mike couldn't tell if he was impressed or bored.

"Can you do it again?" Mike asked, hesitantly. Real magicians never did the same trick twice in a row. The first time, an audience

would be amazed. The second time, the audience would be trying to figure it out. Inside the magic shop, though, magicians were always sharing illusions with one another. That was the whole point of the place. So Mr. Zerlin smiled and said, "Sure."

This time, Mike shuffled the cards. He handed them to Mr. Zerlin, and Mr. Zerlin closed them into the box. He pressed the box to his head again and sighed. "Jack of diamonds," he said, like it was tiring him out to use his psychic powers. He opened the box and pointed—that's how Mike knew he was supposed to take the card out. Jack of diamonds, just as predicted.

Then Mr. Zerlin put the box behind his back. "Queen of hearts," he announced. Of course, it turned out that was the next one in the deck. Mike bet he could identify every card in the box. He watched closely, but he couldn't figure out how Mr. Zerlin did it.

Meanwhile, Cam was pacing around the middle of the store. He kept picking things up, looking them over, and putting them down. A china plate. A dusty accordion. A mirror. Mike noticed that he wasn't going into the section of the store that said *Secrets Inside*. He was sticking to the non-magical merchandise. The "antiques" that were mostly junk.

Without a word to Mike, Mr. Zerlin put the box of cards on a shelf and stepped away to talk to Cam. Mike couldn't hear what they were saying because their voices were low. What would a magician say to a card player? Mike wondered. They did totally different things. How did they know each other, anyway?

"Did you meet Cam?" asked Carlos, one of the high school kids who worked at The White Rabbit. He was unwrapping a roll of quarters to put in the register. "Cam used to be part of Mr. Zerlin's act," Carlos told Mike.

"Mr. Zerlin's act?" Mike asked. He didn't know Mr. Zerlin had an act! "Where can I see that?"

"Oh, you can't see it anymore," said Carlos. "Without Cam, his show fell apart. Mr. Zerlin's been working on something new, I think." He shrugged, and Mike knew what he meant. No one ever *really* knew what Mr. Zerlin was doing.

"So, what happened?" Mike said. "I mean, Cam seems okay to me."

Their conversation was cut off when the door opened and a woman came in, holding a little girl by the hand. Carlos had to help them, so Mike was on his own.

Not that he minded. He loved learning stuff from Mr. Zerlin or the other magicians who came to the store. But he also learned a lot from just hanging around and listening. Some of it was magic—that was how he'd figured out how to do a rising card trick, where he could make the card that someone selected rise magically out of the deck. Mike had also learned some non-magical stuff. He was pretty sure that Carlos had a girlfriend, for instance. That had to be why he was always texting when he thought that no one was watching.

Mike went into the *Secrets* room and took a deep breath. He'd only known about it for a few months, but this was his favorite place in the world. Every time he came here, it felt like his birthday. So what was he going to do? Every inch of the room was crammed with shelves and bins of magical gear to try out.

Today, Mike was drawn to one of the bookshelves. He wasn't much of a reader, but books were a good way to learn about new kinds of magic, right? There they were, lined up by category. Stage illusions. Close-up magic. Mind magic. That must have been what Mr. Zerlin just did, Mike thought.

Below those titles was a row of books labeled History of Magic. History? No way Mike was reading that. But he'd heard Mr. Zerlin talk about studying the old masters of magic. Even the ones who took their secrets to the grave. Like, say, Harry Houdini. The greatest magician of all time.

Houdini's original name had been Erik Weisz, which he changed to Weiss before he changed it to Houdini. Weiss as in Mike Weiss!

Hey, Mike realized. This was his chance to find out if there was any connection to his family. Suddenly, Mike was *all about* history.

The only problem? These books weren't written for kids. So many long words! So many long chapters! Mike wished Mrs. Canfield could see him now. He worked really hard trying to read the thickest one.

He made it through a detailed description of one of Houdini's most famous escapes, where the magician was handcuffed and locked inside a container filled with water. When the book described how Houdini changed this act over time though, Mike's attention wandered. He flipped to the section of black-and-white photos in the middle.

There was Houdini jumping off a bridge. There he was with his wife, Bess. There he was onstage at a show. Mike loved looking at the shocked expressions on the people in the audience. There he was with a whole group of magicians.

Then Mike noticed a detail he'd missed.

Houdini was at the end of the line of magicians, standing in front of a bench. A hat was perched on the bench's arm, right beside him. Maybe it was the latest accessory for fashionable gentlemen in 1917, but Mike didn't think so.

He thought it was Houdini's magic hat.

Why? Well, Mike just happened to have a magic hat in his closet at home. It was about the same shape as the one in the picture. A little lopsided, and drooping on one side. And that hat had a label inside that said "E.W." Which happened to be Houdini's initials before he changed his name.

It was warm in the windowless room, but Mike had goose bumps.

Luckily, he was in a place that sold all kinds of old stuff. He walked out into the antiques area and grabbed a magnifying glass that was next to a giant dictionary. Carefully, he peered through it at the picture.

The hat in the photo was a perfect match with the hat in his closet.

Mike had wondered if Houdini was connected to his family. And here was the answer, right in front of him, he was pretty sure.

Then the alarm on his watch bleeped. Mike had to go.

Mr. Zerlin was still whispering with Cam, and Carlos was still helping the lady and the little girl. Mike waved, but didn't say good-bye. He'd be back, and they knew it.

Mike biked home as usual, but it felt like he was flying.

That was *his* magic hat in the old-school magicians' picture.

And that little fact, like the wave of a wand, could change everything for Mike.

Chapter 3
FAMILY TREE

The next morning, Mike was eating cereal at the kitchen table in his pajamas—an old soccer jersey and a pair of ripped shorts—when his back door swung open. "Hello?" a voice said. It was his next-door neighbor, Nora, carrying her backpack.

Mike wanted to shrink under the table. "What are you doing here?" he asked with a mouthful of Honey-Nut Cheerios.

"My parents had to get to work early today, so I'm supposed to wait here till it's time to leave for school," Nora said. "Sorry, they worked it all out with your mom."

Nice of her to tell me, Mike thought.

He said, "I just need to get dressed," rushing out of the kitchen. If he went fast enough, maybe Nora wouldn't notice that his shorts had a hole in the butt.

When he came back, ready for school, she was drawing a picture in her notebook. Even without seeing it, Mike knew it could go in a museum. That was the thing about Nora. She was good at everything she tried. She was probably the smartest girl in fourth grade. She could out-run any kid on the playground, even the boys. She was a piano prodigy and she could walk on her hands. Mike wasn't usually friends with girls. Especially girls like Nora. But she was an only child just like him, and

they spent a lot of time together. Mike had decided she wasn't that bad.

Nora turned the page on her masterpiece. On the next page, Mike could see a lot of writing. He poured himself another bowl of Cheerios and slopped some milk into it.

While he chewed, Nora said, "I'm working on some questions to ask my Uncle Terry."

"Oh," Mike said blankly. "Is he coming to visit?" Nora's relatives all lived in California or something. A long way from their town in Maine.

"No, I'm interviewing him on the phone," Nora explained.

"Why are you interviewing your uncle again?" Mike asked. Had she told him already?

"For the family history project." Nora said. From his look, she could tell he was clueless. "The whole fourth grade is doing it this month. I bet you'll get the assignment today."

This was always happening to Mike. At first, he thought that teachers were sharing their lesson plans with Nora. That didn't even surprise him. Then he realized that the three fourth-grade classes always had the same assignments. Mrs. Canfield's class was always a little behind the others.

A family history project? So convenient! Something Mike actually *wanted* to learn about in school!

"So what do we have to do?" he asked her.

"First, we have to interview someone from our family," Nora said. "It's best if it's not our mom or dad, but someone from an older generation. We'll collect stories and pictures from them. We'll make a family tree and a family map. Finally, we'll map all of the families in our grade."

"Sounds cool," said Mike. He already knew who he'd interview. His grandma, who'd given him the hat.

Since he'd already heard about the assignment, Mike tuned out when Mrs. Canfield introduced it to the class. Sometimes, he struggled to follow along while a million other ideas flew through his head. It was nice to be ahead of everyone else, for once. When Mrs. Canfield handed out a worksheet with a picture of a tree on it, Mike knew what to do.

He'd call his grandma tonight, he decided. Set up a date, and ask her to find an old photo album. If she had a picture of the magic hat, he might be able to see its owner.

Mrs. Canfield clicked to the next slide. "The stories we gather will be powerful," she said to the rest of the class. "We'll get to know our families a little better. And we'll get to know ourselves a little better, too."

Mike was supposed to be writing down her directions. He had a notebook in front of him and a pencil in his hand. On the paper, though, he tried out that math trick that Mr. Malone had showed him. It was just like the tutor said. If he picked a three-digit number and followed all the steps, he always ended up with 1089.

But how could that be?

"What's that?" a voice whispered. Mike looked up. Oscar was watching.

"Just a . . . math game," Mike whispered back.

"Can I play?" said Oscar.

Mike shook his head. He didn't want to get in trouble. "Maybe later," he said. But it was too late.

"Mike, do you have something you'd like to share with the class?" the teacher said.

"Not really," mumbled Mike. Everyone was watching him again.

Oscar, though? No one gave him a second thought.

After a while, Mrs. Canfield broke the kids into pairs. They were supposed to come up with questions to ask in their interviews. But before Mike could sit with his partner, Mrs. Canfield called him over.

She looked at him with concern. "Everything okay?" she said. "Still on track?" That was a code they'd made up at the beginning of the year. If Mike got off track, it meant that he needed a short break to work off some energy and collect his thoughts. Mrs. Canfield would let him leave the room and walk down the hall. Much better than disrupting the class, she said.

"I'm fine," Mike said. "Oscar asked me a question, and I answered him."

"I understand," said Mrs. Canfield, her mouth in a straight line. "Think you can stay on track till lunchtime?"

She thought it was all his fault!

All right . . . so he wasn't really paying attention. But nothing would have happened if Oscar hadn't opened his big mouth! Mike's parents said that Mrs. Canfield was firm, but fair. How in the world was this fair? he wondered. After that, it was hard to focus on his work.

Ten minutes before lunch, Mrs. Canfield gathered the class back together. "Before you go downstairs, I wanted to let you know what to expect," she said. She sounded sorry that she was delivering bad news. "You'll find there are some new rules in the cafeteria. Nobody wants another food fight."

"It wasn't a food fight!" Lacey insisted.

"Lunchtime needs to be orderly," said Mrs. Canfield, "so everyone can refuel."

She called them new rules, but all the kids could tell what they really were: a punishment. Usually the fourth graders could sit anywhere they wanted in the cafeteria. For the next week, though, they could only sit with kids from their class. No big deal if you had some good friends in your class. If you didn't, you were out of luck.

Naturally, all of Mike's good friends had Mrs. Dorr or Mr. DeCamilla.

He stomped down the stairs to lunch.

So Zack and Charlie got to sit together, as usual. Mike saw Nora laughing in the middle of a bunch of girls. Adam was standing in the hot lunch line with a kid from his class. Even Jackson Jacobs was doing just fine. He'd taken up three chairs at Mr. DeCamilla's table, and no one was going to stop him.

Where did that leave Mike? Well, he could sit next to Oscar, he figured. Maybe he'd

apologize for getting Mike in trouble. But Will snagged the seat before Mike could get there, and no one scooted over to make room for him. The boys were all together in one big clump, and the best Mike could do was settle into a place on its edge. Right next to know-it-all Emily.

Mike took a deep breath. That was what he was supposed to do if he felt like he was going to explode.

Then he remembered something. People would treat him a whole lot better when they found out about his family tree.

Chapter 4
FAMILY PICTURES

Mike's grandma lived too far away for him to bike to, so his dad was driving him over for the interview.

In the front seat, Mr. Weiss was humming along to some old song. In the backseat, Mike was tapping his foot like crazy. He was really nervous. Soon, it could be—as a magician might say—the moment of truth.

Houdini never had any kids, so Mike couldn't be Houdini's great-great-grandson or anything like that. He had to be related to Houdini in some other way. If anyone knew what it was, his grandma would. He felt a little funny asking her, though. It was like saying, "Please tell me how I am related to royalty." And what if he had it all wrong?

Mike's dad turned into the driveway and stopped the car. "Say hi to Grandma for me, okay?" he said, unlocking the doors.

"See you in half an hour," Mike said. His dad was squeezing the driving between two important meetings. But Mike wouldn't need that much time. Half an hour was way longer than he'd ever spent on any school project. He hopped out of the car and ran to his grandma's front door.

She was there before he even rang the doorbell, wrapping her arms around him and hugging him fiercely. Mike already knew one thing

about his family tree: Grandma was his favorite person on it.

When she finally let him go, Mike spotted an open suitcase on the hallway floor. There was a big straw hat on top of all the clothes.

"Where are you going?" Mike asked.

"It's finally time for the cruise!" she said.

Every year, Grandma went on a Caribbean cruise with her sister, Mike's great-aunt

Carol. "I don't leave till tomorrow, though," she added.

Mike grinned. "You're bringing me back a T-shirt, right?" he said. That was another thing she did every year.

"Of course!" said Grandma. She led Mike into her living room, telling him about her trip. "We'll stop at four islands," she explained. "The ship has seven decks and five swimming pools. Can you believe it? Next year, you'll have to come with us!"

She sat down in one corner of her flowered couch and picked up a yellowed photo album. "I've been looking forward to our talk all day. So, how should we start?" she asked.

Mike took Mrs. Canfield's tree worksheet, a little crumpled, out of his pocket. "At the beginning, I guess," he said. There was a leaf on the tree for every member of Mike's family. He needed basic information about each person. First, he'd do what he had to do. Then he would ask about Houdini.

"What year were you born?" he began.

"1940," she replied.

"And where?" he asked. How could he not know that?

"New York City," she said. "My family lived with my grandfather until I was five."

Carefully, Mike wrote "New York" on the sheet. Grandma's grandpa would be his great-great-grandfather, right? There was a place for him on the family tree, too.

"What was your grandfather's name?" he asked.

Grandma looked embarrassed. "I don't know what his real name was, actually," she said. "He came over from Hungary and changed his name to Theo Hardeen."

Mike gulped. "Harry Houdini was from Hungary," he said casually.

"Really? How interesting!" said Grandma. Nothing more.

Mike tried to stay focused. He couldn't get into that yet. What else did he need for the tree? He asked, "What did your grandpa do for work?"

"He was pretty well known in our neighborhood," his grandma recalled. "I remember my mother pointing out his name on a sign outside a theater one night. I felt so small, in such a big crowd. I looked up, and all I could see were the legs of the other people, waiting in line."

She didn't actually answer his question. And then her phone rang.

"Excuse me, Mike, but I need to get that," she said. "Just one second ..."

He waited while she talked. "Oh, yes, it would be great if you'd water the plants when you feed the cat!" Mike's grandma told the caller. "Could you bring the mail in, too?"

Mike got right back to his questions when she hung up. "So, your grandpa was an actor?" he reminded her.

Grandma shook her head. "There weren't many movies back then. He was in a kind of variety show. Vaudeville, it was called. There were several different acts in a row. Dancing, juggling, magic, singing, comedy . . ."

"He did *magic?*" Mike said. "Like Harry Houdini?"

"I suppose so," Grandma began. She was cut off by the sound of the doorbell.

This time it was a neighbor, dropping off a book for Grandma to read on her trip. Mike tried to be patient while he watched the clock on the wall. The minutes were ticking away.

Finally, Grandma closed the door and returned with the book. "Where were we?"

"Your grandparents?" Mike said.

"Oh, yes," said Grandma. "Once we moved, I didn't get to see them very often."

"So, where did you actually grow up?" Mike asked, his pencil ready.

"A small city called Appleton, Wisconsin," Grandma replied. "A long way from New York."

Mike knew all about Appleton. "That's where Harry Houdini grew up!" he told her.

"Is that so?" said his grandma.

And then they were interrupted again. Mike couldn't believe it.

This time, Great-Aunt Carol was on the phone, calling to iron out some last-minute details. Why were grown-ups always so busy? Mike wondered. First his dad, and now his grandma. All he wanted were some answers about his family!

Mike paced around the living room, then checked out the pictures on Grandma's mantelpiece. There were his parents on their wedding day. There were his cousins, Jake and Lily, at a parade. There was Mike, in his school picture from last year.

Grandma's photo album was still sitting where she left it. Mike could look at those pictures, too! He picked up the album, blew the dust off the cover, and took a look inside.

He turned the brittle pages as carefully as he could. Most of the pictures showed two little girls. Grandma and Great-Aunt Carol? Mike wondered. He would ask, except Grandma was still gabbing on the phone. Mike saw pictures of a new puppy, a birthday, a trip to the beach. They were all starting to blend together. Then a newspaper clipping fluttered out.

The caption was torn off, but the photo showed two men in a street, posing in front of a shop window. The one on the right was tall, with curly hair cut short. The one on the left was smaller and very muscular—the ink was

MARTINKA'S FINE MAGICAL APPARATUS & ILLUSIONS

smudged around his face. From their clothes, Mike guessed this picture had been taken before his grandma was born.

First, Mike noticed the name of the shop: Martinka's Fine Magical Apparatus and Illusions. It had to be a magic shop! Just like The White Rabbit!

Then Mike saw that the shorter, stronger man was holding a tall, black hat. It dangled from his hand, by his side.

And that hat? Even though it was upside down, Mike could see that it didn't quite stand up straight.

Mike was so excited, he could have jumped off the couch. It was *his* hat! So who was the guy?

He could be some random magician, right? Mike told himself. He could be someone who worked at that store. He could be trying to sell the hat. He might not be in Mike's family at all.

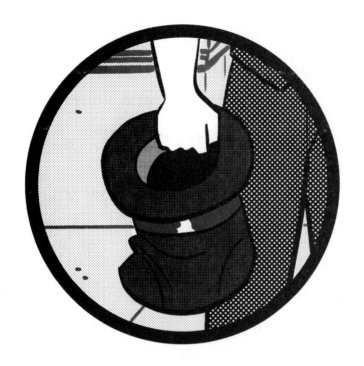

But then why would he be in the photo album? Mike wondered.

Who else could it be?

Well, it could be E.W.

Also known as Harry Houdini.

Grandma finally finished her call and turned to him. "Mike..." she said, starting to apologize. But Mike didn't even mind. He just wanted to know.

"Grandma," he said urgently, pointing to the photo. "Who's this?"

She lifted the clipping, and squinted. "The one on the right is my grandfather," she said. "I'm not sure of the other one."

"Do you see what he's holding?" Mike said, jabbing at the picture. "It looks like my hat! You know . . . the one you gave me! You said it belonged to a cousin or something?"

"My favorite cousin," said his grandma. "He used to do magic tricks when we were little. That's not him in the picture, though."

"But what if someone else had the hat *before* your cousin?" Mike asked. "There's a label in it that says E.W. They must be someone's initials. Is there anyone else who could have owned it first?"

"I don't think so," said Grandma, shaking her head.

Mike couldn't stop. "But what if it was the man in the picture? I need to know who he is! It's really important for my family tree project," he said.

Not to mention my reputation at school, he thought.

Grandma frowned. "I wish I could tell you, Mike," she said.

Mike was desperate to know the whole story. "Is there anyone else you could ask?"

There was a knock at the door. His dad.

"Tell you what," said Grandma. "Let me bring the clipping on the trip. Carol's memory is much better than mine. I bet she'll recognize him in an instant."

That wasn't what Mike wanted at all. But his dad was at the door, pointing to his watch.

The final answer would have to wait.

.·˙.×.ₒ* **Chapter 5** .·×✳ₒ*
FIELD TRIP

So Mike didn't know the details yet. He didn't know *for sure*. But there were all these coincidences: Hungary, vaudeville, Appleton. And Houdini's hat was right there in his family photo album! Mike was only one step away from discovering where Houdini fit on his family tree.

It was hard to think about anything else.

The family tree worksheet would be due soon, but Mike couldn't finish filling it out yet.

What was he supposed to do until he heard from Grandma? He had to hand in something, right? He didn't want Mrs. Canfield—or the kids in his class—to think he was blowing it off.

He wrote on some of the leaves, and made a list of questions to ask his parents some other time. What were the names of his second cousins? Where was his other grandma born? He would do as much as he could.

Mike sighed. He'd had enough of this for today.

He crept downstairs to stuff his papers in his backpack for the morning. If he got them in there quickly, his mom and dad wouldn't ask to check them over.

A lucky break! They were folding laundry in the den. "Oh, can you take this basket upstairs?" his dad asked.

"Sure," Mike said brightly. "No problem." Once he did it, he was free!

Now, for the most important part of the day. Not school, not sports, not music, not friends. For Mike, the most important part of the day was studying a giant book, a gift from Mr. Zerlin, called *The Book of Secrets*. It contained directions for every magic trick that Mike had ever seen or dreamed of. *The Book of Secrets* looked like it had been passed down from magician to magician for a hundred years. Actually, Mike thought it might be magical itself.

He closed his eyes, flipped through the pages with his fingers, and let *The Book of Secrets* open on its own. It had a way of knowing just what he needed to read.

He blinked and looked at what he'd chosen. Pretty freaky!

The magic trick on this page was called "In My Mind's Eye." It was the same one Mr. Zerlin had done for him and Cam at The White Rabbit!

Mike put on his desk lamp and read the directions carefully. He'd need to cut a tiny window in a box of cards, just big enough to show the number and suit of the top card. The rest of the illusion would depend on keeping the window hidden.

With a pair of scissors, Mike made the window and worked through the trick. His audience was a stuffed bear sitting on his bed. He showed the bear the box of cards, keeping his thumb over the window. Then he took the cards out of the box and handed them to the bear to shuffle. Okay, the bear couldn't exactly shuffle like Cam. After a moment, Mike took the cards back and explained what was happening next.

"With my mind's eye, I will see the top card in the deck," Mike told the bear. "My mind's eye" was a fancy way of saying "my sixth sense" or "my magic powers."

He lifted the box toward his forehead with the window facing him. Just like Mr. Zerlin, he acted like he was thinking hard. The trick was to glance so quickly through the window that no one would notice. Well, he managed to fool the bear!

He ran through it several more times, but there was a problem with this trick. He couldn't practice it in front of a mirror, like he usually did. He couldn't watch himself watching the window!

Mike wasn't ready to perform this one in public. But he could test it out on Nora, then show it to Mr. Zerlin at the shop. He wondered how much Houdini practiced to get things right.

As part of their family tree project, the whole fourth grade was taking a field trip to visit the

In My MIND'S EYE

*T*HIS IS ANOTHER ILLUSION THAT REQUIRES A LITTLE ADVANCE PLANNING.

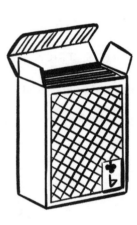

 1.

BEFORE YOU BEGIN, YOU'LL WANT TO CUT A SMALL SQUARE WINDOW IN THE BOTTOM RIGHT-HAND CORNER OF A BOX OF CARDS, ON THE SIDE OF THE BOX WHERE THE FLAP FOLDS IN. IT SHOULD BE JUST BIG ENOUGH TO SHOW THE NUMBER AND THE SUIT OF THE TOP CARD.

 2.

YOU'LL BEGIN BY SHOWING YOUR AUDIENCE THE CLOSED BOX OF CARDS. AS YOU DISPLAY IT, YOU'LL KEEP YOUR THUMB OVER THE WINDOW YOU'VE JUST CUT.

3. NOW, TAKE THE CARDS OUT OF THE BOX AND HAND THEM TO A SPECTATOR. HIS JOB WILL BE TO SHUFFLE THE CARDS AS MUCH AS HE LIKES.

WHEN HE'S FINISHED, YOU'LL PUT THE CARDS BACK IN THE DECK, WITH THE FACES OF THE CARDS TOWARD THE SECRET WINDOW.

LIFT THE PACK OF CARDS TO YOUR FOREHEAD, WITH THE WINDOW FACING YOU. QUICKLY GLANCE AT THE WINDOW—YOU'LL HAVE TO BE CAREFUL AND QUICK ABOUT THIS. TELL YOUR AUDIENCE THAT YOU'LL SEE THE FIRST CARD IN THE DECK IN YOUR MIND'S EYE. WHAT'S THAT? A MYSTERIOUS SIXTH SENSE THAT IS NEVER WRONG!

5. NAME THE CARD, OPEN THE BOX, REMOVE THE CARD . . . AND AMAZE THE AUDIENCE.

NOW THE NEXT CARD IN THE DECK IS VISIBLE THROUGH THE WINDOW. YOU CAN DO THIS TRICK AGAIN AND AGAIN!

archives of a local museum. It wasn't too far from school, so all three classes walked into town together, even though it was about to rain.

Mike had no clue what an archive was until Mrs. Dorr explained it to the group. "The archives are where many important local records are kept," she said. "Records of who bought and sold houses in town, for instance, over the past two centuries. Who was born and who died. Can anybody tell me how this could be useful in creating a family tree?"

Not me, Mike thought, stepping away.

Of course Nora knew. "We could find the exact dates of big events in our families' lives," she said. Mike, standing next to her, could feel the warmth of the teachers' smiles.

Mrs. Canfield added, "Even if your family hasn't lived in this town for long, you'll still find some of this information useful. Once you know what to look for, we can help you find facts about your own family, wherever it originally comes from."

Mike raised his hand. "What if your family is originally from Hungary?" he asked.

Before he could hear the answer, Jackson Jacobs was already mocking him. "Yeah, I'm hungry, too!" he cackled. "Who brought the snacks?"

"Just ignore him," Mike's friend Adam said, standing next to him.

But it wasn't that easy. For the whole walk, Mike kept his head down and tried not to attract Jackson's attention.

The museum was in an awesome building on the edge of the college campus where Mike's parents worked. It had a round tower on one side and a wall of stained-glass windows on the other. It looked a little like a castle and a little like a church, Mike thought. Inside, it was

so cool and quiet that everyone piped down for a while.

In a hushed voice, the museum director showed the fourth-graders around. There was a collection of old maps, some photos of the town the way it used to look, and a bank of computers where some of the kids could search for records.

The problem? It was a really small museum, and there were a lot of kids.

Mike wasn't the greatest about waiting, but he braved a long line for the computers. Then, just as he was about to sit down, a thick arm shoved him out of the way and said, "My turn!"

No, it wasn't Jackson. It was worse.

One of those tough twins from Nora's class—Tyler or Chase, he couldn't tell who was who—slid into Mike's seat.

"Hey!" Mike said. But no grown-ups were watching. So what were his choices? Give the kid his place. Or push him back where he came from . . . in front of the whole fourth grade.

Yeah, Mike knew he should stand up for himself. But if there was a problem, people might think he had started it. Same old story.

So Mike stepped away, Tyler-or-Chase settled in front of the screen, and Jackson muscled his way toward his pal. "Game on!" he yelled, and suddenly, video laser blasts were ringing out across the quiet museum. They'd closed out of the museum's Web site, and now they were playing a game.

Mrs. Canfield rushed over to find out what had happened. She headed straight for Mike.

"He cut in front of me," Mike said quickly. "I had nothing to do with it."

Mrs. Canfield believed him. She turned to the twin and snapped, "What on earth do you think you're doing, Tyler? You'll need to

discuss this with Ms. Scott when you get back to school."

But Tyler cut her off. The principal? He couldn't care less. "It's not like Mike was gonna find anything in the local records," he said.

Jackson was smirking right beside him. "Yeah, his family is from Hungary."

Mike's temper flared. Was that supposed to be some sort of insult? he wondered. Why wouldn't Jackson just leave him alone? And what was wrong with Hungary, home of Houdini? Suddenly, Mike felt a surge of family pride.

Mrs. Canfield sputtered, "That doesn't mean you can . . ."

Mike was the second kid to interrupt her in the past three seconds. "Tyler's right," he said to his teacher, like he was above it all. "I mean, I don't really need to look at the museum site, anyway. I know all about my family tree already. I'm from the same family as Harry Houdini, you know."

It was as good as true, Mike thought. He just *knew* it.

Jackson Jacobs rolled his eyes. "Right," he said. "Show me."

"Fine," said Mike. "I will."

Game on.

✦ Chapter 6 ✦
A FAVOR

Mike had a spring in his step, as his grandma might say, all the way back to school. It was raining for real now, but Mike splashed happily into every puddle he passed. Jackson wasn't with the rest of the fourth grade. Tyler, either. Mr. DeCamilla had walked them back to school before everybody else.

Right now, they'd be sitting in Mike's usual spot outside Ms. Scott's office. Hopefully feeling worried, he thought. The school secretary, Mrs. Warren, always gave Mike a treat while he waited—she liked him. She probably hid the candy jar in her desk when Jackson arrived, though.

So he had a whole afternoon without the fourth-grade bullies breathing down his neck. And when Mrs. Canfield's class got back to the classroom, there wasn't even time for her to start a new lesson!

She recapped the field trip. Then she said, "Anyone want to play Seven-Up?"

Mike always loved a reason to put his head on his desk. But today he had another idea.

"I have a question, Mrs. Canfield!" he said. Before she reminded him to raise his hand, Mike blurted out, "What if I did a magic trick? And *then* we played Seven-Up?"

"Yeah! A magic trick!" the rest of the class chimed in.

RISING *from* *the* DECK

$\mathcal{F}$OR THIS TRICK, YOU WILL NEED ONE DECK OF CARDS, DIVIDED INTO 2 PILES, WITH 26 CARDS IN EACH PILE. BEFORE YOU PERFORM THIS TRICK, YOU WILL NEED TO PREPARE SOME SPECIAL CARDS. MAGICIANS CALL THESE GIMMICKED CARDS.

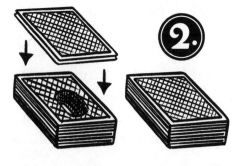

1. TO MAKE THE GIMMICKED CARDS: HOLD A CARD LENGTHWISE, FACEDOWN, WITH YOUR THUMB CENTERED AGAINST THE BACK. DRAW AROUND THE THUMB WITH A MARKER, THEN CUT EACH CARD ALONG THE MARKER LINE WITH A PAIR OF SCISSORS. YOU'LL NEED TO DO THIS WITH 24 CARDS, THEN STACK THEM ALL ON TOP OF ONE ANOTHER, FACING DOWN.

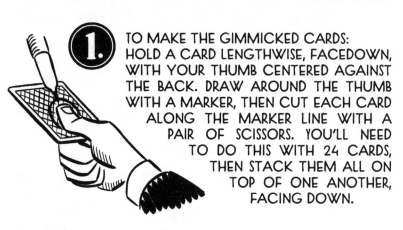

2. PUT TWO UNCUT CARDS ALSO FACEDOWN ON TOP OF THE GIMMICKED CARDS. SO, ONE PILE OF CARDS WILL HAVE 24 GIMMICKED CARDS AND 2 UNCUT CARDS. THE OTHER PILE WILL HAVE 26 UNCUT (UNGIMMICKED) CARDS. HAVE THE TWO PILES SIDE BY SIDE. NOW, YOU'RE READY TO START!

HAND THE UNGIMMICKED PILE TO SOMEONE IN YOUR AUDIENCE, EXPLAINING "THIS HALF IS YOURS, AND THIS HALF IS MINE." THE SPECTATOR SHOULD GO THROUGH HIS HALF AND PICK OUT A CARD AND REMEMBER IT.

NOW, TELL THE SPECTATOR TO PUT HIS HALF OF THE DECK DOWN, WITH HIS CHOSEN CARD ON TOP. YOU WILL PUT YOUR HALF OF THE DECK — THE GIMMICKED HALF — ON TOP OF THAT.

PICK UP THE DECK, WITH THE CARDS FACING THE AUDIENCE. SAY YOU'RE GOING TO MAKE THIS DECK A LITTLE LIGHTER, BY REMOVING TWO CARDS FROM THE FRONT (THE CARDS FACING THE AUDIENCE) AND TWO FROM THE BACK.

THIS MOVE IS A DISTRACTION, THOUGH. WHILE YOU ARE DOING THIS, INSERT YOUR FINGER INTO THE BOTTOM OF THE GIMMICKED CARDS AND USE IT TO PUSH THE SPECTATOR'S CARD — THE TOP ONE IN THE UNGIMMICKED DECK — SLOWLY UPWARD OUT OF THE DECK. "IS THIS THE ONE YOU PICKED?" YOU'LL ASK.

BEWARE: THE SPECTATOR MAY BE SPEECHLESS.

Mrs. Canfield nodded. "Wonderful," she said. Mrs. Canfield could be hard on Mike, definitely. But she also liked to encourage her students' interests.

Mike always had a couple of tricks prepared, things he could do without a lot of advance notice. "In my Mind's Eye" wasn't ready to go yet, but he had something else up his sleeve.

He had to be careful, because this trick involved what magicians called gimmicked cards—ones he'd changed so they were different from other cards. It was important not to let anyone see them. But Mike had practiced this illusion a million times in front of the mirror. He was pretty sure he had it down.

The special deck of cards was in the pocket of his sweatshirt. He took it out, divided it into two piles, and put them on a desk in the front row. Then he called Will over. "This half of the deck is yours," he said, pointing. "And this one is mine."

Will nodded. "Got it."

"Here's what you need to do. Pick one card out of your half, and remember it," Mike said. "But don't tell me what it is." Will looked through his cards. "Ready?"

When Will said, "Ready," Mike went on.

"Now, put your half of the deck down, with the card you chose on top." Mike put his half on top of Will's half, and picked up the entire deck of cards.

"Man, these cards are kind of heavy," Mike said. "I think I'll just take a couple of them out of the pile." He removed two cards from the front of the deck, and two from the back. As he did it, though, something strange happened. The queen of diamonds started poking out from the middle of the deck, rising slowly and eerily away from the other cards.

"That's weird," said Mike. "Is this the card you picked?"

Will's eyes bulged out. "Weird? That's amazing!" he told Mike.

The other kids crowded around. "How did you do that?" they all said at once. "Can you show us?"

All eyes in the class were on him again. But this time, it was for a better reason.

Nora was waiting for Mike at their meet-up place after school.

"Where were you?" she asked.

"Just running late," he said. Or maybe lingering till he was sure that Jackson had already left.

Nora's mom would worry if they didn't get home quickly. "So, what happened at the museum? Did you see that Jackson and Tyler had to leave early?" she asked, beginning to walk.

It was embarrassing to tell other kids when he he got picked on. Today though, Mike had the upper hand.

"Tyler cut in front of me in line for the computer, and started playing video games! And then Jackson made fun of my family. But I got him to shut up, for once," Mike said.

"No way!" said Nora. "Good going!"

"Yeah, I told him I didn't need to use the computer anyway. I already have plenty of stuff to put on my family tree. I found out I'm related to Harry Houdini!" It felt truer every time Mike said it.

Nora stopped. "You're related to Harry Houdini? Really?!"

"Yeah," Mike said modestly. "My grandma told me all about it." More or less.

"So, how are you related?" Nora asked. "Like, where does he go on your family tree?"

"Well, I'm still trying to figure that out," admitted Mike.

"Didn't your grandma say?"

"She wasn't sure, either. She has to check with her sister. They just left on a cruise."

Nora paused. "Then how do you know?" she asked.

"I just know," Mike said.

"For sure?" said Nora, confirming.

Mike avoided her eyes. "There are a lot of coincidences, okay?"

He knew he could prove it. The hat, the book—what more could he need? He'd show Jackson, all right. But Nora's help would make or break his plan.

Mike trusted Nora with all his magical secrets. Could he also trust her to handle her mom?

♠ ♠ ♠

Nora's mom believed there was a right way and a wrong way to do everything.

The right way to spend time after school was homework first, everything else later. And the right way to host a neighbor kid—like Mike—was to make him stick to the routine. Mike had never even thought of breaking her rules. But Nora was taking charge.

Mrs. Finn was at the kitchen table, wearing glasses and going through a stack of papers. "Hi, you two!" she said cheerfully.

"Mom," Nora said, all business. "We have an emergency."

Mrs. Finn looked alarmed. "Nothing bad," Nora rushed to add. "Mike needs to get something downtown...for an assignment," she explained.

"Downtown? Where?" her mom asked.

Nora glanced at Mike, like "told you so." Her mom would never say no if it was an emergency for school.

"I know it sounds strange, but we actually need to go to an antiques store," Nora said.

Then she moved in with the bait. Her mom was really into yoga and healthy foods. "Right next door to that new smoothie shop you wanted to check out. Remember?"

Twenty minutes later, Nora's mom was ordering a kale and carrot smoothie, and Mike was headed to The White Rabbit with Nora. He wondered if Houdini had a partner like her. Mike owed her, big-time.

He practically sprinted into the store, leading the way to the back room. Where was that book about magical history? "It's the thickest one," Mike told Nora, remembering. With that and the hat, he'd have evidence for Jackson. Solid proof.

"Here it is!" Nora said, plucking it off the shelf.

Mike flipped through the pictures until he found Houdini with his hat. "See?" he showed her. "It's a perfect match with mine!"

Nora looked at it closely. "They do look alike." she said.

"Jackson will flip when he sees it!" Mike predicted. Now, he just had to get the book out of the store.

Mike didn't like asking Mr. Zerlin for a favor. But what else could he do? He didn't have enough money to buy the book. He thought back to all those times he'd begged his parents for a cell phone. What he really needed was a credit card!

Mr. Zerlin was on a stepladder in the front window. It looked like he was changing the display for the first time in, like, a decade. Late-afternoon sun was streaming through the window that used to be dusty and dirty. Where there was once a grimy bunny—a not-quite-white rabbit—there was now an extra-large magic hat, all lit up like it was onstage.

"Mr. Zerlin?" said Mike uncertainly.

Mr. Zerlin climbed down the ladder. "What can I do for you, Mike?" he said.

Mike explained as fast as he could. "I was just wondering if I could borrow this book till tomorrow. I mean . . . I know you don't usually loan things out. But I can't buy it and . . . I just need it for one thing. Please? I promise I'll bring it back tomorrow."

Sometimes, Mr. Zerlin was mysterious and distant. Sometimes, he said things that no one could understand. This afternoon, though, he was perfectly clear and direct. "Not a problem, Mike," he said. "My pleasure."

Mike's eyes popped open with surprise. He didn't think it would be that easy.

Mr. Zerlin dropped his voice and spoke magician to magician. "I trust you with my secrets!" he said. "After that, a book is nothing. See you tomorrow."

⋅ ˟ ✳ Chapter 7 ⋅ ✳ ⋅ ✳
AVOIDING JACKSON

Mike couldn't sleep. Usually, one of his parents had to wake him up after his alarm clock went off twice. Not today, though. He lay in his bed and watched the sun rise.

Today, he'd bring the book and the hat to school to show Jackson. But what if they weren't enough? What would Mike do if Jackson didn't believe him?

A part of him wished he'd never said anything at the museum. Maybe it would have
been better to let Jackson get his way, just like
he always did. Did Houdini ever have to deal
with bullies? Mike wondered.

He kicked off his covers and went downstairs. He could hear his dad shaving in the
bathroom beside the kitchen. Mike waited till
he came out in his bathrobe.

"Hey, Dad," Mike asked casually, "do you
think I could call Grandma while she's
gone?"

His dad seemed surprised. "You could try, I
guess. She probably has her cell phone with
her. But you can't be sure there's service wherever she is. The ocean is a pretty big place," he
added. Like that was news to Mike.

"Maybe I could e-mail her?" Mike said
hopefully.

"Same problem," his dad said. "I know you can get e-mail on a ship, but I'm not sure it's that reliable."

Mike decided to do both. When he called his grandma's number, it went right to voice mail. "Grandma, it's Mike," he said after the beep. "Just wanted to make sure you remembered to talk to Aunt Carol. Who's that guy in the picture? It's super-important!"

In the subject line of his e-mail, he wrote "A reminder!" The message was short and to the point.

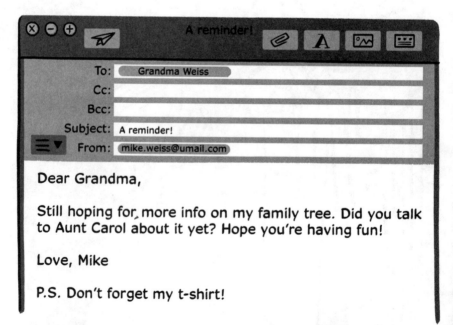

To: Grandma Weiss
Cc:
Bcc:
Subject: A reminder!
From: mike.weiss@umail.com

Dear Grandma,

Still hoping for more info on my family tree. Did you talk to Aunt Carol about it yet? Hope you're having fun!

Love, Mike

P.S. Don't forget my t-shirt!

Mike's mom came downstairs and said, "You're up early!"

Yeah, Mike thought. And it's going to be a long day. Even with his proof in hand, he didn't feel like seeing Jackson. Maybe it would be better to stay home.

Mike's friend Zack had told him about a foolproof method to fake being sick. While his parents were getting dressed, Mike poured himself a special drink: a tall glass of milk and orange juice mixed together. As soon as he drank it, Mike was guaranteed to puke. First, he had to make his head feel really warm. That way, his parents would believe he had a fever.

Zack held a hot lightbulb up to his forehead, he remembered, but Mike didn't want to burn himself. Instead, he turned his mom's hair dryer on high and blasted it at his face.

COOL COINS

START OUT BY SHOWING YOUR AUDIENCE FOUR COINS, A MARKER, AND A HAT. YOU CAN USE ANY COINS, BUT THEY SHOULD BE FOUR OF THE SAME COINS.

TIP: LARGE COINS, SUCH AS QUARTERS, WORK BEST.

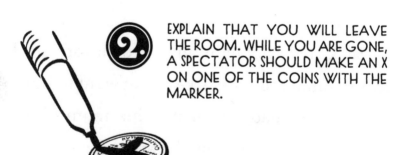

2. EXPLAIN THAT YOU WILL LEAVE THE ROOM. WHILE YOU ARE GONE, A SPECTATOR SHOULD MAKE AN X ON ONE OF THE COINS WITH THE MARKER.

AFTER THAT'S DONE, THE SPECTATOR SHOULD HOLD THE COIN IN THEIR FIST AND BRING IT UP TO THEIR HEAD, CONCENTRATING ON THE MARKED COIN. THEN THAT SAME COIN SHOULD BE PASSED TO SEVERAL OTHER SPECTATORS WHO SHOULD ALSO HOLD THE COIN IN THEIR FIST AND CONCENTRATE ON THE COIN AS WELL.

WHEN THEY'RE FINISHED, THE FIRST SPECTATOR SHOULD PUT ALL OF THE COINS —INCLUDING THE MARKED ONE —INTO THE HAT AND CALL YOU BACK IN TO THE ROOM.

 WHEN YOU RETURN, YOU'LL PUT YOUR HAND INTO THE HAT AND PICK OUT THE MARKED COIN WITHOUT EVEN LOOKING!

YOU DON'T NEED YOUR SENSE OF SIGHT FOR THIS TRICK. YOU NEED YOUR SENSE OF TOUCH. QUICKLY PICK UP, HOLD, AND RELEASE EACH COIN. THE COIN THAT'S BEEN HELD BY THE SPECTATORS IS STILL WARM —THAT'S HOW YOU KNOW IT'S THE ONE WITH THE X. THE OTHER COINS WILL FEEL COOL!

His mom banged on the bathroom door before he could drink the drink. "What's going on in there?" she asked. "Why are you using my hair dryer?" Then she saw the glass perched on the edge of the bathroom sink. "Bleeeck," she said, picking it up. "What is that? Please don't drink that, honey." Before Mike could take it back, she poured it into the toilet.

Mike ended up walking to school with Nora as usual. He carried the hat and the book in one of those cloth shopping bags from the grocery store.

But Jackson didn't tear past Mike and Nora on their walk. He didn't push Mike out of line on the playground before school. He didn't scowl when their classes passed each other in the hallway. He wasn't at lunch, and nobody missed him. Without Jackson Jacobs, actually, the whole fourth grade got compliments on their good behavior in the cafeteria. "Keep this up," said Ms. Scott, "and we'll return to our usual seats in no time!"

Mike found Nora on the playground at recess. "I guess Jackson's absent," Nora said.

"Do you think he got expelled?" Mike asked. "That was pretty bad, playing video games in the museum."

"We can only hope," said Nora.

After lunch, Mike's class split into three reading groups. While Mrs. Canfield worked with one of them, the other two were supposed to be working independently. Emily Winston's group was writing down the answers to some questions. Mike's group, though, was chatting. As usual. Annabelle said, "I loved that magic trick you did, Mike! Where did you learn to do that?"

It's in my genes! Mike thought. Soon his reading group would know all about it.

"Well, I go to this magic shop sometimes," Mike told her. "And they've taught me lots of stuff. And I watch magicians on YouTube, and go to magic shows when I can. Oh, and I practice constantly. And I read books sometimes, too."

Will lowered his voice. He made sure that Mrs. Canfield wasn't watching from the back corner of the classroom. "Could you show us another trick?" he asked.

Mike didn't want to get caught, but he couldn't resist. Would Harry Houdini ever turn down an opportunity to perform? Not a chance.

He couldn't take out Houdini's hat without attracting Mrs. Canfield's attention, but he had four quarters and a crushed-up cap in the fleece vest he was still wearing from recess. That would be enough.

"Does anyone have a marker?" he asked quietly. Will handed one to Mike.

"Great," said Mike. Now he explained what was going to happen. "I'm going to go out to the water fountain, and you guys are going to use the marker to make an X on one of these coins. Then, one by one, you each need to do this with the marked coin, okay?"

He scrunched a coin up in his fist and raised it to his forehead to demonstrate. "That way you can send me a mental message. Drop all four coins in the hat when you're done.

When I come back into the room, I'll know which one has the X!"

He glanced over at Mrs. Canfield, but she was absorbed in her group's work. Hopefully, she wouldn't notice the other kids squeezing the coin.

"A mental message?" asked Lacey.

"You'll see. Just wait. It's amazing!" Mike said. "Mrs. Canfield, may I please be excused?" he called out.

He took his time, walking to the bathroom and back. Then he peeked into the classroom, just to make sure things were going right.

Will was holding the coin to his forehead like Mike had shown him. What he didn't know was that Mike could identify the marked coin by its temperature. After everyone in the group had squeezed it, the marked coin would be hotter than the other ones in the hat.

Mike returned without saying a word. He took the knit cap from Lacey and put one hand inside. Right away, he could tell which coin it was, but he made a show of picking the quarters up one at a time. "Is it this one?" he asked, raising his eyebrows suspiciously. "Or is it this one? No, it must be this one!"

Mike held up the coin in triumph, showing the whole group the X.

And Mrs. Canfield? She was in a long discussion with her group. She hadn't seen a thing.

Annabelle high-fived Mike, and Will whistled under his breath. It was like Mike could see something new in their eyes. Respect, maybe? Magic worked magic for Mike.

Mike was so swept up in being the center of attention that he didn't notice the knock at the door, or the face in the window, until another kid stepped into his classroom.

It wasn't unusual for students from other classes to come in and out, delivering messages from other teachers.

But why in the world would any teacher give Jackson Jacobs that job?

Jackson swaggered in holding a rolled-up map. "Hey, look who it is!" he said with a sneer. "Little Houdini!" He looked over at Annabelle and Lacey, sitting beside Mike. "Showing the girls a little hocus-pocus, huh?" Annabelle blushed and Mike's hands clenched into fists. Not that he would actually punch Jackson. But wouldn't it feel great if he did?

Something silver was glinting in Jackson's mouth. Braces! Could that be where he was all morning? The orthodontist? More evidence that Jackson really belonged in junior high.

Mrs. Canfield came out of the corner. "Can I help you, Jackson?" she said.

"Mr. DeCamilla wanted me to deliver this," Jackson said. "For the family tree thing."

When her back was turned, Jackson got in Mike's face. "I'm still waiting for your . . . information," he hissed.

"After school," said Mike. No point in saying where. Jackson would find him, wherever he was.

Before the bell rang, Mike got onto the class computer. He logged into his e-mail account and held his breath. Still nothing from his grandma. Oh well, Mike thought. He had enough to put Jackson in his place.

⋆ Chapter 8 ⋆
FACING JACKSON

By the time Mike left the building, the last kids were filing onto the last school bus, and Jackson was dribbling a basketball furiously on the playground. When he saw Mike, he leaped up and stuffed it into the basket.

Jackson stalked right over to him. "Got the goods?" he snapped.

Mike swallowed hard. Jackson was always a bully and a pain in the neck, but now he was

angry, too. Maybe because Mike had landed him in the principal's office? His expression was as friendly as a rabid dog's. His braces looked sharp and threatening.

You have this, Mike told himself. Just do it already.

Mike opened his shopping bag and took out his hat. "This is my magic hat," he informed Jackson. "Handed down through the generations in my family." Or close enough, he thought.

Carefully, keeping the secret pockets hidden, he showed Jackson the label.

"E.W., see?" Mike said. "It stands for Erik Weisz. That was Houdini's real name, before he changed it."

"So?" Jackson said.

"So," replied Mike, "the hat belonged to Harry Houdini. Who handed it down to some cousin, who handed it down to me."

"Yeah, okay," Jackson said. He didn't sound convinced.

"But that's not all," Mike went on.

Next, he took out the history book from The White Rabbit. He turned the pages till he got to the photos, and lifted the book up about ten feet until it was in front of Jackson's eyes.

"See that picture?" Mike said. He'd marked it with a sticky note. "That's Houdini, right there. And see what's next to him?" He paused to let it all sink in. "My hat."

"Looks just like every magic hat I've ever seen," Jackson said. He shrugged and pushed the book back at Mike.

"No way!" Mike said. "See how it's all lop-sided? It's definitely mine. That's how I know Houdini's in my family. For sure."

Jackson squinted at Mike.

"Seriously?" he said. "Are you joking? This is your proof? You're even dumber than I thought."

Mike felt his face turning red. He felt the sting of a few tears, too, but he bit his tongue to stop them. Nothing would be worse than crying in front of Jackson.

Why couldn't Jackson see it? The connection was perfectly clear to Mike.

There were all those coincidences, he thought. Should he try to explain them?

No, he decided. Instead, for some reason, Mr. Zerlin popped into his mind. What would he say? The words escaped Mike's mouth before he could swallow them. "You've got to believe."

That was it. Jackson's patience broke. "You've got to be kidding me! Let me tell you something, Weiss. You have nothing here. Some messed-up hat and a library book you can't even read. You? Related to Houdini? Not in a million years!"

He knocked the book out of Mike's hand, and when Mike bent to pick it up, Jackson

snatched it. "Your Uncle Harry did escapes, right?" he said. "Well, who's escaping now?" He tore off into the trees at the edge of the playground, yelling, "Come and get me!"

Jackson hadn't touched him, but Mike felt like he just got beat up. And who knew where he was hiding? Jackson lived in Mike's neighborhood, so Mike could run into him anywhere between here and home. What would he do then? Was there anyone who could help?

What would Houdini do if he were me? Mike wondered. What would Mr. Zerlin do?

Mr. Zerlin. Oh.

What would he say about the missing book?

Mike picked up his shopping bag, put on his backpack, and dragged himself across the playground. This was a disaster. Why couldn't his grandma just clear things up once and for all? Why did he ever go bragging to Jackson? And why did Mr. Zerlin dare to lend him a book, anyway? Didn't he know who he was dealing with? Mike lost things all the time. You might even call him a loser.

So, now what?

If Mike didn't return the book, Mr. Zerlin would never teach him another magic trick.

And without magic, Mike would *really* need a new reputation at school.

Mike kicked the gravel on the path. No way he was coming back here in the morning. He'd have to do that milk-and-orange-juice trick every day from now till the end of the year. Nora could bring him his homework. Or maybe he could be home-schooled. He'd never have to see Jackson again.

"Mike?" said a voice from the monkey bars. "Are you okay?"

Mike froze. Was it Jackson? No, it was Nora. On top of the bars with a book.

"What are you doing?" Mike asked.

"Waiting to walk home?" she said, like it was obvious. But she was obviously lying, because she must have been watching him. And she was still here, waiting. Man, she really had his back.

"That didn't go so well," Mike said. To put it mildly. "Did you see?"

"Yeah," she said.

"He didn't believe me. And he took my book," Mike told her. His voice quavered a little. "I mean, Mr. Zerlin's book."

Even with Houdini's genes, Mike had no clue what to do now. It wasn't like some magic trick could bring the book back. And what if he didn't have Houdini's genes at all? What if his family tree was just like everybody else's? Boring and normal.

"So, what are you going to do?" Nora asked. Mike was annoyed, even though she was trying to be nice.

"You tell me," he said. He couldn't tell her he was dropping out of fourth grade.

"We could go to The White Rabbit," she suggested.

"No way!" said Mike. "What for?" So Mr. Zerlin could find out about the real Mike? The one who caused trouble wherever he went?

"Mr. Zerlin is expecting you," Nora pointed out, the way a grown-up would. "And you need to tell him what happened."

Mike didn't want to do it, but she was right.

There were practical problems, though. Like how were they going to get there? His parents weren't about to drive him, not even if he bribed them with a smoothie. They'd say he could go on his own. But what would he do with Nora, then? He couldn't just leave her home with his mom.

Nora wasn't a magician, but she could still read his mind. Or at least the expression on his face.

"Maybe you have a better idea," she said. "But I was thinking I could ride my bike."

It must be great to be Nora, Mike thought. She didn't need to earn privileges, she just *got* them. Her parents were really strict about some things, and not at all about others. "Of course they trust me to bike downtown with a friend," Nora said like it was nothing. "Why wouldn't they?"

Why hadn't she told him this before? Mike wondered.

One call to Mrs. Finn confirmed it. "Just make sure you wear your helmet and follow the rules of the road," she told Nora.

The bike ride made Mike forget about Jackson for a few minutes. He and Nora raced down a side street and practiced skidding till they left black marks on the pavement. As they pulled up in front of the magic shop, though, he felt mad all over again.

Mr. Zerlin had trusted Mike with his secrets. He'd trusted Mike with his book. But how could he trust Mike with anything now?

Believe *what*? Mike thought bitterly as he saw the mat out front. He already knew he'd never see the book again. He probably wouldn't be a magician, either, and it was all Jackson's fault.

He wiped his feet on the mat and walked through the door with his head down.

.·. $\times$。$\ast$ Chapter 9 .$\times$ $\ast$。$\ast$

HELP FROM HOUDINI

Mike pushed open the door to The White Rabbit, maybe for the last time.

Carlos was juggling four balls behind the counter. Mike hated to break his concentration, but he needed to get this over with. "Where's Mr. Zerlin?" he asked Carlos. "I really need to talk to him."

Carlos picked the balls out of the air and answered, "He's with Cam. They're practicing."

"Planning a new act?" Mike asked quickly. How great would that be?

"I think so," Carlos said. "But I don't know the whole story. Come with me—they're in the basement." Mike and Nora followed him to the stairs.

Mike had seen Carlos and some of the other teenagers coming up from the basement before, but he'd never been down there himself. He'd figured it was a dark place with a lot of boxes, and maybe a business office. Halfway down, he could see he had it all wrong.

Actually, there were rows of soft chairs, like at a movie theater. There was a stage up front, with a heavy red curtain. There were bright lights rigged up, and a little static coming through some speakers. Right there, in the middle of everything, was Mr. Zerlin.

When he was in the front of the store, ringing up orders, Mr. Zerlin seemed pretty strange.

He had that wild hair, and that mysterious way of speaking. It was like he didn't fit into the usual world. Here on this basement stage, though, he seemed like where he was supposed to be. His smile was so bright that it could light up the basement by itself.

Beside him onstage was a tall wooden cabinet. Mr. Zerlin opened it and gestured, as if an audience was really right there in front of him. Maybe he was deciding where he would stand and what he would do at some future show. He didn't say anything, but Mike could tell—just by the way he moved—he was showing the pretend audience that his cabinet was empty.

Mr. Zerlin closed the cabinet and locked it with a silver key. He turned toward the empty chairs, like he was saying something else to the audience. Then he turned back, put the key in the lock, and opened the cabinet again.

It wasn't empty anymore. Cam was standing inside!

"So, why did Cam leave Mr. Zerlin's act?" Nora asked Carlos, whispering.

Carlos shrugged. "Creative differences. Or something like that. But they're starting to put together something new! I can't wait to see what they come up with."

Mike swallowed a lump in his throat. He couldn't wait to see it, either. But would he?

The stage lights turned off and the regular old basement lights flipped on. Mike was standing there blinking when he heard Mr. Zerlin say, "Mike!" The magician walked over to say hello. He asked "What did you think?"

"G-Great," Mike stammered. "I can't wait to see the whole show."

"All in good time," said Mr. Zerlin. Whatever that meant.

Mike could feel Nora looking at him. Urging him to do what he came to do.

"Mr. Zerlin," he said as bravely as he could. "I have something to tell you. I'm pretty famous for making mistakes, but I just made a big one."

"Everyone makes mistakes," said Mr. Zerlin. "Go on."

So Mike did. "Remember that book you lent me?" he continued. "It was so great that you let me borrow it. And I brought it to school, to show other kids some stuff about those old-time magicians."

He didn't tell Mr. Zerlin about his family's link to Houdini. Bragging about it had got him into this mess in the first place.

Mr. Zerlin waited for him to get to the point.

"So, I thought people would think it was cool. But someone I showed it to—a mean kid, actually—he took it and ran off with it. Now, I

don't know where it is. And I don't know when I can give it back."

Mike choked out that last part, staring at his shoes.

"It will turn up," said Mr. Zerlin. "Just wait and see."

It was the first time that Mr. Zerlin had ever sounded like one of Mike's parents.

Did he even understand how serious this was?

"You don't know Jackson," Nora said. "The mean kid, that is."

"But I do know Mike," Mr. Zerlin said. "And he will find a way."

Mike looked up. What was that supposed to mean? Was Mr. Zerlin mad or wasn't he? Could he ever come back to the store?

Mr. Zerlin was smiling. "You remember Harry Houdini, right?" the magician asked Mike.

"Yes, of course!" Mike said. "I know all about him!" Mr. Zerlin had no idea.

"Houdini may have the answer," Mr. Zerlin suggested.

"But how . . ." Nora started to say.

Cam's voice interrupted. "Let's take it from the top!" he called from the other side of the room as the lights went down again.

"What?" sputtered Nora. "I don't understand!"

Nora was smart, but she didn't think like a magician.

Mike thought he knew what Mr. Zerlin was saying, though. And now he thought he might know how to get the book back from Jackson.

At Mike's house, Nora was still trying to figure it out. "Everybody makes mistakes?" said Nora. "Is that a good thing or a bad thing?"

Mike was feeling upbeat. "I think he meant it was okay," Mike said. "He thinks I can figure out what to do!"

"How can Houdini have the answer?" Nora complained. "He's been dead for almost a hundred years!"

"Maybe Houdini once did something that we should copy," Mike explained. "Or said something that we could tell Jackson."

"Too bad we don't have that book about Houdini," Nora said. "That would really come in handy, right?"

Well, yeah. But Mike had something better. "What about *The Book of Secrets*?" he said.

Nora brightened up. "You're a genius!" she said. A major compliment, coming from her.

Mike took *The Book of Secrets* out of its hiding place, closed his eyes like he always did, and opened the book at random. But he was pretty sure there was nothing random about it, because when he opened his eyes, he was staring at a trick called "The Great Escape."

The GREAT ESCAPE

1.

$\mathcal{F}$OR THIS STUNT, SOME SPECTATORS WILL NEED TO PLACE A BROOMSTICK OR A SIMILAR TYPE OF STICK ACROSS YOUR SHOULDERS, AND YOU WILL NEED TO HOLD YOUR ARMS OUT WIDE, PARALLEL WITH THE STICK. THE STICK SHOULD REACH OR PASS YOUR HANDS. WITH A PIECE OF VERY THICK ROPE, THE SPECTATORS WILL TIE EACH OF YOUR WRISTS TO THE BROOMSTICK. YOU MAY BE UNCOMFORTABLE, BUT IT WILL ONLY LAST A MINUTE.

2. WHEN YOU'RE READY TO PERFORM, ASK TWO SPECTATORS TO HOLD UP A CURTAIN, ONE ON EACH SIDE, IN FRONT OF YOU AND HAVE THEM FACE TOWARD THE AUDIENCE. THEY MAY NEED TO STAND ON CHAIRS OR SOMETHING TO MAKE SURE THAT YOUR SHOULDERS AREN'T VISIBLE. NOTE: ANOTHER OPTION IS TO STEP BEHIND A SCREEN SO YOU WOULD ONLY NEED THE SPECTATORS' HELP FOR TYING THE ROPES.

3.

TO ESCAPE, YOU USE YOUR FINGERS TO NUDGE OR SLIDE THE STICK IN ONE DIRECTION WITH ONE HAND, WHILE PULLING THE STICK WITH THE OTHER HAND, THROUGH THE LOOPS OF ROPE. WHEN YOU CAN GRIP IT WITH AN ENTIRE HAND, YOU CAN SIMPLY PULL THE STICK OUT. THEN LET THE STICK DROP TO THE FLOOR. YOU'LL STILL HAVE ROPE BRACELETS . . . BUT YOU'LL BE FREE!

The description under the title said, "A simple, but dramatic, illusion in the tradition of Harry Houdini."

A coincidence? Maybe. Or magic, just when he needed it most.

"What if we use Houdini's trick to convince Jackson I'm related to Houdini?" Mike said.

"And then he'll give back the book?" Nora asked.

"I think we should try it," Mike decided.

He put on his desk lamp and read the directions carefully. For this stunt, they would need a long stick—like a broomstick—and a couple of pieces of thick rope. Also, a curtain and some people who would hold it up to hide him.

"I can do it," said Nora. "And why don't we ask Adam, too?"

The idea was that the broomstick would be placed on Mike's shoulders, and he would spread his arms out wide as somebody tied it to his wrists with rope. "This stance looks frightening to the spectator," said the book. "In fact, however, the escape is simply a matter of pushing the stick through the loops of rope."

The people holding the curtain would know what was happening, because they could see it. "To the audience, however, the magician completes a dangerous feat in a few seconds flat," *The Book of Secrets* promised.

Mike read on. "Your partner will need to guard your secrets well. The success of your performance will rest, in part, on whom you share it with."

Mike caught Nora's eye. At least he had that part covered. He had the idea, he had the directions, and he had the partner he needed to pull it off. Now, he just had to believe.

✳ Chapter 10 ✳
THE GREAT ESCAPE

The next morning, Mike and Nora carried a lot of stuff to school.

Nora had a king-size bedsheet stuffed into her backpack to serve as a curtain during their performance. Mike had a broomstick he'd taken from his garage, minus the bristles that made it a broom. They had their lunchboxes and backpacks. Mike had his magic hat, too, just for good luck.

They staggered up the street and around the corner, but nothing could weigh Mike down. He'd tricked Jackson before and he would trick him again! He just kept telling himself that. He could do it!

They slipped into school just before the bell.

As soon as he came out for recess, Mike could see that something was happening near the swings. A group of kids was gathered in a tight circle around one boy. He towered above everyone else, wearing a black hat and waving a wand.

If you didn't know better, you might think it was Mike Weiss, looking mean and extra-large. But this morning, there was a new magician in town: It was Jackson Jacobs.

"Abracadabra!" he yelled at the kids who were watching. "Alakazam!" He took his hat off and reached for something inside. It's probably supposed to be a rabbit, Mike thought. Or a flower.

All the kids laughed when Jackson pulled out a pine cone instead. Had it fallen from a tree?

"That's not magic!" someone called out.

Jackson ignored the heckling. "Pick a card, any card," he ordered a second-grader in the crowd, shoving a deck of cards at him. The boy chose one and Jackson said, "Now, don't tell me what it is." He consulted his cheat sheet. "I mean, it's *fine* to tell me what it is." Then he dropped the deck by accident and cards went everywhere. He almost looked upset as he picked them up. "Let's try that again," he said.

Mike hated that feeling of messing up a magic trick. He wondered if it bothered Jackson, too.

"He doesn't know what he's doing," Mike heard one kid whisper.

"Who does he think he is?" her friend said back, "Harry Houdini?"

"He's trying to be like you," Nora told Mike.

That was so weird that Mike didn't even know to respond. And where did Jackson learn how to do magic tricks?

When Jackson caught sight of them, he rushed toward Mike and Nora. "Your book stinks!" he told Mike. "It has no magic tricks at all! I had to look them up online!"

Mike shrugged. "I don't need a book to give me directions," he said. "I don't need to look online, either." He talked down to Jackson, like Jackson always talked to him. "But *you're* not related to Houdini."

Jackson snickered. "Neither are you," he shot back.

He was playing right into Mike's hands. "Fine," Mike replied. "How can I convince you once and for all? What if I do one of his tricks? Handed down through my family?"

Jackson was all over it. "One of those escapes? Yeah. I'd love to see that. Any day now, right?" He cracked himself up.

"And if I do it, you'll give me the book back," Mike added.

Jackson rolled his eyes. "Whatever. It's useless."

Mike pretended to cough so he could cover up his smile. "Meet me right here, after school," he said. "And see for yourself." He turned around and followed Nora to the school's front door.

Mike was not exactly at his most attentive for the rest of the school day. He was so distracted that Mrs. Canfield asked him if he needed to go to the nurse.

Instead, Mike hid out in the teachers' stairwell. He opened his backpack and took out his magic hat. Maybe it belonged to Houdini and—as much as Mike hated to admit it—maybe it didn't.

So what if it wasn't really his family tradition?

And what if Houdini wasn't the key to improving his reputation? The other kids really liked his magic tricks. Even Jackson wanted to do magic now! Maybe it was just going to take some hard work and some time. Like, say, learning to make a card disappear.

"Feeling better?" Mrs. Canfield asked when he got back.

"Much better," Mike said. "Thanks."

The afternoon passed in a blur, though Mike did write one thing in his assignment notebook. "Family trees due tomorrow." He still wasn't sure what to do about that. Wait till his grandma's cruise was over?

As soon as the bell rang, Mike hurried out to the playground to meet Nora. She stood on the blacktop with Adam, who was in her class.

When Jackson arrived, Mike took charge. "This afternoon, Jackson, I will attempt the greatest escape that has ever taken place on this playground," he proclaimed. "It's not one of the escapes that made Houdini famous," he pointed out. "Instead, it's one he did . . . as a child. At family gatherings."

Jackson couldn't tell that Mike was bluffing. He just stood there with his arms crossed, scowling. A crowd of other kids gathered to watch, too.

Mike handed the broomstick to Nora. He turned so his back was facing Jackson, and spread his arms out wide, parallel to the ground. "Nora, will you tie this broomstick to my wrists?" She held it up across his shoulders and took two pieces of thick rope from her pocket.

"Not so fast, Weiss," growled Jackson. "She's in on this trick, right? I think I'll do it myself."

"That's fine," Mike said. "I can escape any bonds." Bonds were knots or other restraints—it was a word Houdini used all the time.

When Mike was all tied up, Jackson walked around him. "Looking good," he said. "Real good."

Actually, it was pretty uncomfortable to stand here like this. Not that Mike would ever let anyone know that. "Ready for me to break loose?" he asked.

"Yeah," Jackson muttered. "You'll still be standing there next week."

"Within a minute," Mike predicted, "I will come out from the other side of the curtain."

Somehow Nora had smuggled out two folding chairs from the gym. She set them up on either side of Mike, then she and Adam stood on the chairs and lifted the bedsheet in front of him. From where Jackson was standing, Mike was invisible.

Jackson started counting, like he was tracking the seconds. "*One . . . two . . . three . . .*"

Mike felt a wave of panic sweep over him, now that he was alone behind the curtain. He and Nora had practiced hard, but what if it didn't work? He took a deep breath to calm himself down. Then he used his fingers to nudge the broomstick through the loops of rope. Jackson had tied them tightly, but the broomstick still slid easily.

"*Ten . . . eleven . . . twelve*," Jackson counted.

When Mike had pushed it pretty far, he could grab it with one of his hands and finish the escape. The rope was still tied to his wrists, but he was free! If he had a good magic word, Mike would have said it now. Just as Jackson hit *fifteen*, though, Mike knocked the curtain down with his broomstick and stood there, holding the stick like a sword.

Nora and Adam acted like they had no idea what had happened. "Free!" Mike shouted. "I'm free!" He was so relieved he forgot, for a

second, that he always knew the trick would work. Did Houdini ever feel that way? he wondered.

The crowd of kids started clapping.

"Just like Houdini," Mike told Jackson. "No doubt."

"Right," Jackson said sarcastically. He always said that.

For a second, Mike was worried. Jackson was acting the way he always acted. What if he wasn't convinced?

While he was still at a loss for words, Mike moved in for his part of the deal. "Now, you owe me a book. Hand it over."

Jackson shoved the book at his chest, like it was no big deal. But Mike noticed he wasn't looking at anyone. Then he walked really fast off the playground. It was definitely a big deal to Mike!

In case it got damaged, Mike didn't stuff the book in his backpack. He wrapped it in the sheet instead, and cradled it in his arm. He and Nora were getting a ride home, so he wouldn't have to carry it far.

Mike was already thinking of how he'd go to The White Rabbit, return it to Mr. Zerlin, and find out more about his new act with Cam. Get back to normal.

It turned out his mom had been parked near the playground while The Great Escape was happening. "What was going on over there?" she asked. "Looked like some kind of show." She'd left early that morning, before Mike packed up all his gear.

"Just some third-grade project," Nora said quickly. Mike's mom didn't want him doing magic at school.

When they got to a red light, Mike's mom passed him something into the back seat. "This came for you today," she said to Mike. "A post-card from Jamaica!"

A Caribbean island. One of the stops on his grandma's cruise.

The family tree project was due tomorrow, and Mike still had some work to do.

Or did he?

Mike's grandma had tiny, neat handwriting, so she could fit a lot on the card. It said:

Dear Mike —

I spoke to Aunt Carol, and you won't believe what she told me!

My grandfather, as I told you, changed his name when he was young. It turns out he had a brother who changed his name, too.

My grandfather, Ferencz Weisz, became Theo Hardeen. His brother, Erik Weisz, became Harry Houdini.

Together, they ran a magic shop — Martinka's — and performed all over the world.

But because Houdini died young — and I barely knew my grandfather — I never knew about this branch on our family tree!

Will tell you much more when I come home! Running out of room...

XOXO, Grandma

p.s. Wait till you see your t-shirt!

Mike's heart raced, like when he played hard in gym class. It was really true. He was related to Houdini! And it was going to change everything.

"Hey, did you read what Grandma wrote?" he asked his mom.

"Actually, no," his mom admitted. "It was a busy day. How's the trip? Any news?"

Well, it wasn't going to change his mom.

He passed the card to Nora, and looked out the window while she read it. The news wasn't going to change things with Nora, either. She'd believed in him all along.

Then, Mike thought of something crazy. What if this news didn't change anything at all?

The kids at school already thought he was related to Houdini. He'd proved it to all of them—and Jackson—right? What more did he have to say?

Mr. Zerlin thought he was powerful, with or without Houdini. Mrs. Canfield didn't care about his family tree, except for his assignment.

So, who was left? Mike wondered. Who could he impress? Himself?

Himself. Not a bad idea. Maybe he was the only who really cared. The only one who'd find new strength in the connection.

Houdini was the greatest magician the world had ever known. And Mike shared some part of his DNA, right? So, how would he carry on his family tradition?

Nora was finished reading. She looked over, smiled, and gave him a thumbs-up.

Mike, in turn, put his hand up, like he was making a promise. To be the greatest magician his neighborhood ... his grade ... his school had ever known!

Hey, he had to start somewhere.

The End

Fourth grade has just started
and Mike's already in trouble.
Then, he and his new neighbor Nora
discover The White Rabbit. . . .

*Learn how the magic starts in the
first book of* **the Magic Shop** *Series!*

Mike's next magic trick—convincing his parents he's responsible enough to ride his bike to The White Rabbit alone—will take something truly incredible!

Don't miss the second book in
the Magic Shop series!

Mike's magic skills are about
to face their biggest challenge yet—
the school talent show!

*Get ready for a sneak
peek at Book Four of*
the Magic Shop *series. . . .*

The
Disappearing
Magician

The fourth graders filed into Mrs. Kavanaugh's room and stood in a row. The first graders observed them, quiet as mice, from their tiny chairs. Who would he be paired with? Mike wondered. The girl in the unicorn shirt? The boy with the glasses?

The classroom was bright and cheerful, with kids' artwork all over the wall. On a table in the back, Mike spotted a jumbo bag of pretzels and two bottles of apple juice. Snacks! Mike thought. The afternoon was looking even better. He clutched the book he'd brought to read to his buddy. Sometimes he liked little kids, like his cousins Jake and Lily, better than kids his own age.

"Welcome, fourth graders!" said Mrs. Kavanaugh. "Are we ready to get started?" She passed around a cardboard box, and each of Mike's classmates selected a name on a piece of paper from it.

When it was Mike's turn, he stuck his hand in the box and read the name out loud. "Lucas?" he asked, scanning the faces in front of him. A boy with long, shaggy hair raised his hand. "That's me!" he called out. He and Mike walked to the snack table together.

Mike took charge of the apple juice, and unfolded his getting-to-know-you worksheet. This was supposed to make the first grader feel at home with him. "Do you have any pets?" Mike asked. "What are their names?"

Lucas just sat there with his mouth hanging open. His two front teeth were missing.

"Maybe we should just start reading," he said. The book he'd brought was called *The Magic Hat*. He was pretty sure a first grader would like it. Mike showed Lucas the cover.

"I knew it!" said Lucas, just about jumping out of his seat. "You're the magician!"

"I do like magic. . . ." Mike admitted.

"I saw you on the playground," Lucas said, "when I was waiting for the bus!"

He must have seen the Great Escape, Mike realized. With that illusion, he'd tricked Jackson Jacobs, the meanest kid in school!

Lucas was really excited. "I saw you in the lunchroom, too!" he insisted. "You're famous!"

Suddenly, Mike felt two feet taller. Famous? He liked the sound of that. Too bad he didn't see what was coming next.

"Could you do a trick for me?" asked Lucas.

Mike looked around the room. All the names had been chosen and all the kids had broken up into pairs. Mrs. Kavanaugh and Mrs. Canfield were moving around slowly, making sure the getting-to-know-yous were going well.

I'm supposed to make Lucas feel comfortable, Mike thought. And nobody said I couldn't do magic. . . .

He was trying so hard to do everything right! When magic was involved though, Mike couldn't help himself.

As usual, he had a deck of cards in his pocket. He pulled the cards out and held the four jacks in front of him, like a fan. "See these jacks?" he said to Lucas. "I'm going to put them right here on top of the deck."

"Okay," said Lucas, watching.

Mike put the four jacks on top of the deck and lifted the first one off again. "Now, I'm going to place this jack someplace inside the deck," he said. He stuck it in with the other cards, at random, and continued, "I'll do that with the other jacks, too."

Next, he handed the deck to Lucas. "Can you hold these for a second?" When Lucas got hold of them, Mike said, "Now, take the four cards off the top for me, okay?"

Lucas's jaw dropped as he peeled off four jacks in a row.

"Voila," said Mike, scooping the cards out of his hands and wishing, like always, that he had a good magic word. "The four jacks jumped to the top!"

"That's sick," Lucas said, in awe.

Mike looked over at Mrs. Canfield. She was talking to Oscar and heading in their direction. Mike stuck the cards back in his pocket.

"I think we should start the book now, okay?" he said to Lucas.

When their time was up, Lucas didn't want to say good-bye. "See you next week, buddy," Mike said, with a light punch to his shoulder. Lucas beamed, and for a minute, Mike felt like he really was famous.

Mrs. Canfield's class trooped back upstairs just as the end-of-the-day announcements began. Mike was only half listening, as usual. If there was anything important, his parents would tell him.

"Now, for some news that will brighten the dark winter days!" Mrs. Warren, the school secretary, said cheerfully. "On Monday, we will start putting together our first-ever talent show!"

A talent show? The announcement was like an electric shock.

Now, Mike was listening hard.

Mrs. Warren continued, "Bring your act, ready to perform, to the gym after school on Monday afternoon. This is not an audition, but an open call for acts. We will spend the week rehearsing, with the big show Friday night!" Then she moved onto another announcement about the Lost and Found.

Mike wasn't always into school activities. And, okay, it wasn't like anyone was begging him to join the school clubs. But he actually had a talent, the kind he could show onstage! Chess Club kids couldn't say that, could they?

Some people, like Lucas, had seen Mike's magic already. But he could do so much more! What if he didn't have to steal time during class? What if he had a stage all to himself? Then he'd really be famous! Just like his distant relative, Harry Houdini.

Suddenly, the coming weekend was full of purpose. Mike would pick out his best magic, practice with Nora, plan his show.

It was time to get his act together!

Thank you for reading this FEIWEL AND FRIENDS book.
The Friends who made

possible are:

Jean Feiwel, *Publisher*
Liz Szabla, *Editor in Chief*
Rich Deas, *Senior Creative Director*
Holly West, *Associate Editor*
Dave Barrett, *Executive Managing Editor*
Nicole Liebowitz Moulaison, *Production Manager*
Lauren A. Burniac, *Editor*
Anna Roberto, *Associate Editor*
Christine Barcellona, *Editorial Assistant*

FOLLOW US ON FACEBOOK OR VISIT US ONLINE AT
MACKIDS.COM.

Our books are friends for life.